Samuel French Acting Edition

Holly Down in Heaven

by Kara Lee Corthron

SAMUELFRENCH.COM SAMUELFRENCH.CO.UK

ISBN 978-0-573-70197-9

www.SamuelFrench.com
www.SamuelFrench.co.uk

FOR PRODUCTION ENQUIRIES

United States and Canada
Info@SamuelFrench.com
1-866-598-8449

United Kingdom and Europe
Plays@SamuelFrench.co.uk
020-7255-4302

Each title is subject to availability from Samuel French, depending upon country of performance. Please be aware that *HOLLY DOWN IN HEAVEN* may not be licensed by Samuel French in your territory. Professional and amateur producers should contact the nearest Samuel French office or licensing partner to verify availability.

For all enquiries regarding motion picture, television, and other media rights, please contact Abrams Artists Agency, 275 Seventh Avenue, New York, NY 10001 Attn: Leah Hamos.

MUSIC USE NOTE

IMPORTANT BILLING AND CREDIT REQUIREMENTS

HOLLY DOWN IN HEAVEN received its world premiere production presented by the Forum Theatre at the Round House Theatre in Silver Spring, Maryland on October 3rd, 2012. The production was directed by Michael Dove, with sets by Steven T. Royal, props by Debra Crerie and Kathryn Rzasa, costumes by Denise Umland, lighting by Brittany Diliberto, and sound by Thomas Sowers. The Production Stage Manager was Stephanie Junkin. The cast was as follows:

HOLLY . . . . .Maya Jackson
MIA . . . . .Dawn Thomas
DAD . . . . KenYatta Rogers
YAGER. . . . . Parker Drown
DR. MCNUTHIN . . . . Vanessa Strickland

CHARACTERS

HOLLY – African American, 15, dresses like a missionary. A know-it-all, full of attitude

MIA – African American, 25. HOLLY's tutor

DAD – African American, 40. Handsome, but a little nerdy

YAGER – White, about 18 or 19. Probably good looking, but not too bright

DOCTOR – Female, Off-stage voice

***DR. MCNUTHIN** – A lap dummy

*The other characters are all dolls and will require either off-stage live voices or some voiceover recordings.

TIME

Late 2000s

SETTING

A basement somewhere in the suburbs

Scene One

(In darkness: **HOLLY** *leads* **MIA** *into the basement.)*

HOLLY. OK. This won't be easy *('specially 'cuz I've noticed you aren't exactly what I'd call graceful)*, but you're going to have to keep up with me *and* watch your step. Here we go.

*(***HOLLY** *turns on a light and the audience can now see the basement. There are few actual furniture pieces – a bed, a lounge chair, maybe a small table. The room is mainly a doll museum. There are three huge display cases full of dolls.)*

If you'll follow me to the left here, these are all my latest ethnics. They're all black. The Dolls of the World Barbie collection – Nigerian, Jamaican, Kenyan and Ghanaian and the super-rare Dasia doll, one of the few full-figured fashion dolls in existence. As in all cases, those still in perfect condition (and the only way to be in perfect condition is to be NRFB) are worth the highest value. Certain NRFBs bought today will all be worth tens of *thousands* in about a decade –

MIA. Sorry, what does NRFB mean?

*(***HOLLY** *sucks her teeth.)*

HOLLY. Yeah, can you please save your questions until I'm finished? We have a lot of ground to cover.

*(***HOLLY** *doesn't wait for an answer.)*

HOLLY. Great. Moving forward –

DR. MCNUTHIN. *(She sounds a lot like Carol Channing.)*

(off stage) Show her the Victorian collection. She looks like a college girl. Academic types like old-European shit!

*(***HOLLY** *clears her throat.)*

DR. MCNUTHIN. *(cont.)* Yes, like I said, moving forward. On this wall, you'll see a hodgepodge of American Girls, Precious Moments, Cabbage Patch and a few randomites not even worth mentioning. They're mostly gifts from well-meaning, but ignorant relatives. Several have at least one visible flaw so I saw no point in leaving them pristine. They aren't much more than decoration right now, but someday I may take them to a refiner, who will get them as market-ready as they can possibly be. Then they might be worth a dime or two.

MIA. Are you –

*(**HOLLY** glares at her; **MIA** stops herself and timidly raises her hand. **HOLLY** ignores her raised hand. **HOLLY** walks to the final case.)*

HOLLY. These are my favorite on-displays! My *Asians*! And my very, very, *very* favorite: my Japanese bisque tea server! You'll notice that she's standing on a music box and if you wind her up she'll –

*(**MIA** raises her hand again and waves it around in the air fiercely. **HOLLY** stares at her.)*

Uh-huh. I've been blessed with the gift of sight so yes. I see you. But if you'll kindly think back, say two minutes ago, I believe I politely asked you to *save your questions*!

*(**MIA** puts her hand down.)*

Great. As I was saying –

DR. MCNUTHIN. *(off stage)* You didn't show her the Victorians?

HOLLY. As I was saying –

DR. MCNUTHIN. *(off stage)* What about *me*?!

HOLLY. *(quickly:)* AS I WAS SAYING IF YOU WIND HER UP SHE PLAYS A PRETTY LULLABY AND WILL TILT HER HEAD WHILE POURING IMAGINARY TEA INTO THE LITTLE CUP IN HER HAND!

(pause)

She's priceless. Though her loveliness has been marred by human hands. I suppose that's enough for now.

*(**MIA** raises her hand again. **HOLLY** stares at her. Finally, she points at her.)*

HOLLY. Yes? Mia?

MIA. Are you OK?

HOLLY. Let's keep all our questions on topic, please.

(pause)

MIA. What does NR – ?

HOLLY. Never Removed From Box.

MIA. Are you going to sell all these one day?

*(**HOLLY** laughs, the dolls laugh.)*

HOLLY. Of course not. I just like to keep my dolls at the top of their worth.

MIA. How long have you been out of school?

HOLLY. Is that a tour-related question?

MIA. How long have you been in the basement?

HOLLY. Now you're being hostile.

MIA. Aren't dolls considered false idols?

(The dolls gasp.)

HOLLY. *(Quietly:)* I don't worship them. So no. Is this part of your lesson plan? Mocking my beliefs.

MIA. No.

HOLLY. Then maybe you should stick to what *is*. My father's paying you by the hour. Playtime is over. Get to work.

MIA. You have to take an active part, too, you know.

HOLLY. If you're good at your job, that won't be an issue.

*(Pause; **MIA** gets out some textbooks from her bag.)*

MIA. You're only fifteen?

HOLLY. If you start to pity me, I'll be forced to murder you, mummify you, and turn you into a life-size, and they're very rare. I learned how from a book I read about

Tutankhamen. No one will ever believe I did it 'cuz I'm so young and innocent and adorable!

MIA. That didn't sound like a very born-again Christian thing to say.

(Pause; **HOLLY** *looks worried.)*

HOLLY. You're right. You're here to test my faith. Obviously. I will pass this test. But don't you pity me. I'm warning you.

MIA. I don't.

HOLLY. Good!

MIA. I just meant that you're very smart. For your age.

HOLLY. Oh.

I guess you're more accustomed to the juvenile delinquent type. That's not me. *I* was in spectra. *I* was in G & T.

(pause)

Do you know what G & T stands for?

MIA. Gifted and Talented.

HOLLY. Were *you* in G & T?

MIA. Look. I try to be as blunt as you are yourself so I hope you don't mind my asking: when are you due?

HOLLY. April.

MIA. Then we better get busy.

*(***MIA** *hands* **HOLLY** *some paper and a pencil.)*

We'll start with some Algebra.

HOLLY. Do you need your hearing checked? I just said I was in *Spectra.*

MIA. Pardon me. I forgot I was in the presence of the gifted. Maybe we'll start with some history then. Just until I can catch up with your brilliance.

HOLLY. I didn't say I was *brilliant.*

MIA. *(genuine:)* You didn't have to.

DR. MCNUTHIN. *(off stage)* So the interloper gets to stay?

HOLLY. Yes. Be quiet now.

*(**MIA** looks at **HOLLY**, but doesn't say anything.)*

Scene Two

*(**HOLLY** is dusting the dolls on the ethnics shelf with utmost care.)*

BLACK DOLL. You show too much goddamn favoritism.

HOLLY. We don't say "gd" in this house.

BLACK DOLL. Shiiit.

BLACK DOLL 2. That ain't the issue! We talkin' 'bout your fa-vor-i-ti-sm. Don't act like you don't know what we mean!

HOLLY. I don't.

ALL BLACK DOLLS. Awww! / Shiiit! / Get outta here! / You a liar!

BLACK DOLL. You a Asia-file.

HOLLY. Ohhh! You're jealous of my Asians! Well…yeah. I have no defense there.

BLACK DOLL 2. So you admit it! You a racist 'gainst your own people!

ALL BLACK DOLLS. YEAH!

HOLLY. You're not people. You're rubber, bisque, porcelain, plastic, and cloth. You're possessions. Not people.

BLACK DOLL 2. That make you the overseer?

HOLLY. No. I'm the mistress.

BLACK DOLL 2. One night while you sleep, while you dream a your Mama or indiscretions with sweaty adolescents – BAM! We will Nat Turner your ass!

*(**HOLLY** takes the box holding **BLACK DOLL 2** down from the shelf.)*

Wait! What're you doin'?

HOLLY. I just thought you might be happier. In *storage*!

BLACK DOLL 2. N-no! Please! I was just kiddin' ya! You know I love you, gurrrrl!

HOLLY. Maybe you and all your buddies would like to make the move to STORAGE!

ALL BLACK DOLLS. NOOO! / Please! / Have mercy on us! / We'll be cool!!

HOLLY. Well then, what do we say?

(Pause; they all grumble.)

HOLLY. Let me *hear* it!

ALL BLACK DOLLS. We love you Holly Brannigan. God's everlasting light shines through your beautiful eyes.

HOLLY. Yeah. Um. How 'bout we try that again. With *every*body.

ALL DOLLS IN THE BASEMENT. We love you Holly Brannigan. God's everlasting light shines through your beautiful eyes.

HOLLY. You all are so lovely!

DAD. *(from off:)* Holly?

HOLLY. Oh no.

*(**HOLLY** places **BLACK DOLL 2** back on the shelf.)*

BLACK DOLL 2. Ouch!

You gonna pay one day. I never forget a dis!

ALL BLACK DOLLS. Yeah!

HOLLY. SHHH! If we don't say anything, maybe he'll just leave.

(They all are quiet.)

DAD. *(still off.)* Bubble?

(pause)

Holly Bear?

DAD. *(nothing)* Holly Hobby?

(nothing)

Holly-Wally Doodle?

HOLLY. How DARE you?!

*(**DAD** enters with a paper bag.)*

DAD. Sorry, Bubble! Just wanted to make sure you were still breathin' down here. You used to like that, ya know.

HOLLY. I *never* liked that! You just *tell* me I did.

(Pause. **HOLLY** *continues dusting.)*

DAD. Tutor been by yet?

HOLLY. Not today.

DAD. Oh that's right. Monday, Wednesday, Friday. Wish I could afford to get her here everyday, but that was...If I was *partner*, then . . .

HOLLY. What's in the bag?

DAD. Something special. Something sweet. Something for my pretty little spit bubble!

HOLLY. What?

DAD. Oh nothing. Just a Japanese Wagasa Geisha Doll.

*(***HOLLY** *gasps.)*

HOLLY. In her original case?

DAD. Of lacquered wood and glass.

*(***HOLLY** *squeals.)*

HOLLY. But – But – But how? Where did you *find* her?

DAD. Little thing called E-bay!

HOLLY. E-bay? But that's so simple.

DAD. Sometimes life's a snap, Holly Bear.

HOLLY. Daddy! Have I told you lately that I love you?!

(She leaps at the bag, but **DAD** *holds it away from her, putting himself between her and the bag.)*

DAD. Not yet. Have a little patience there, Bubble. What's the lesson Daddy taught you about special treats that just appear outta nowhere when it's not your birthday and it's not Christmas?

*(***HOLLY***'s face falls.)*

HOLLY. Oh. Everything has a price.

DAD. Good girl. Have a seat.

HOLLY. I'd rather stand.

DAD. I'd like you to sit.

HOLLY. I'd like me to stand.

DAD. I'm the father! You're the daughter! You have to sit down.

HOLLY. I'm a young person! You're an old person! Maybe *you* should sit down!

*(***DAD** *finally sits.)*

DAD. Daddy's just playing. Don't get yourself so upset, Holly-Wally –

HOLLY. Don't say it.

DAD. Somebody's a little cranky today! Maybe it's time for a little nap? Or a CapriSun? I got the Strawberry Kiwi kind!

HOLLY. *Dad*!

DAD. All right! You may have Miss Wagasa Geisha if you'll do what Daddy thinks is best…and talk to our good friend Dr. Markowitz.

(silence)

HOLLY. Get out.

DAD. Holly –

HOLLY. That's the meanest thing you've ever said to me.

DAD. Daddy's little drama queen.

HOLLY. You're a butcher!

DAD. Oh, for Chrissake!

HOLLY. I keep telling you I'm a serious Christian now! I DON'T NEED THIS SHIT!

DAD. Any other girl in your situation would be praising Mr. Jesus Christ if they had a father like me. Understanding! Forgiving! And willing to pay a small price to make it all go away! But no. Not you.

HOLLY. That's right. *Not* me.

*(***DAD** *sighs.)*

DAD. It's abortion, Holly Bear. Hardly genocide. Be a Christian if you must. But don't be a moron.

HOLLY. I'm going to pray very hard for you. Harder than usual.

DAD. Save your breath. I don't want you praying to some Stone Age God on my behalf.

HOLLY. He'll forgive you, though.

DAD. If your Mother could hear you talking like –

HOLLY. She'd be proud of me. And you know it. Who was the one that always took me to church? Hmm?

(no response)

A little louder.

DAD. *(clenched jaw)* Your Mother.

HOLLY. Correct. She'd be beaming with just enough pride for it not to be a sin yet. If you say anything otherwise, you're going to Hell.

DAD. So *you* get to decide that?

HOLLY. No. I can just tell. Because I'm God's favorite.

DAD. Bubble, you're a sweet girl and cute as one a your dollies here, but I don't think you're quite a saint.

HOLLY. I know. God loves them, too.

DAD. Your *dolls*?

HOLLY. *(eye roll)* The saints. They're equal to me in His eyes. Lots of people can be equal to me if they try really hard. They just can't rise above me. In His estimation. See?

(pause)

DAD. Daddy thinks it's time for you to move back upstairs. This whole religious banishment to the basement for your sins is kinda cute, but you're gettin' a little…time to move back upstairs.

HOLLY. No way! Not until the baby comes!

DAD. Holly, I think you're buggin' out!

HOLLY. I know this must be hard for you to *understand* –

DAD. Try impossible.

HOLLY. Seeing as how you weren't exactly Ivy League material in your day – but there is a higher method at work here. I give God this sacrifice, he rewards me in the end.

DAD. What "sacrifice?" Depriving the world of your presence?

HOLLY. No. Depriving myself…the world. *That's* my penance. It'll all work out in the end.

DAD. You're not keeping that baby, Holly.

HOLLY. With prayer, the whole baby issue will be resolved.

DAD. I'm not kidding.

HOLLY. I'm not getting an abortion. I'm not kidding about *that.*

DAD. I know somethin' else you're not gettin', either.

*(**DAD** indicates the paper bag and starts back up the stairs.)*

HOLLY. Daddy?

(He pauses at the top of the stairs.)

Can I at least see what she looks like? Up close?

DAD. If you change your mind, you can see her anytime you want.

*(**DAD** exits. **HOLLY** angrily goes back to cleaning.)*

DR. MCNUTHIN. *(off stage)* Holly?

HOLLY. What?

DR. MCNUTHIN. *(off stage)* Come get me.

HOLLY. I don't feel like it.

DR. MCNUTHIN. *(off stage)* Yes you do. You know you'll feel better if you just do it.

*(**HOLLY** slams the rag down. She exits in the back. We hear her going through things, maybe knocking things over.)*

DR. MCNUTHIN. *(off stage)* Ow!

HOLLY. *(off stage)* Sorry.

DR. MCNUTHIN. *(off stage)* Don't apologize unless you mean it.

*(**HOLLY** reappears with **DR. MCNUTHIN*** and sits her down on a doll-sized wicker chair that clearly belongs to **DR. MCNUTHIN**.)*

DR. MCNUTHIN. *(cont.)* Where are my glasses?

HOLLY. Where did you leave them?

DR. MCNUTHIN. Honey, I can't walk without the help of humans! *You* must have put them somewhere.

*(**HOLLY** looks around and finds a small pair of glasses and places them on **DR. MCNUTHIN**'s face.)*

DR. MCNUTHIN. Well?

HOLLY. I hate him! Do you know what he wants me to do?

*(**HOLLY** lays down on the couch with her head near **DR. MCNUTHIN**.)*

DR. MCNUTHIN. Yeah.

HOLLY. That's so horrible! How can he want that to happen to his grandchild?

DR. MCNUTHIN. You took college prep biology! You know you don't have a child in there yet.

HOLLY. That's academic, though. I'm talking from the soul.

DR. MCNUTHIN. You're talkin' from your rear.

HOLLY. I don't want to do tough love.

DR. MCNUTHIN. Have you thought about how you're gonna take care of a kid?

HOLLY. Sing to it, feed it, put powder on its butt.

DR. MCNUTHIN. I learned something when I was getting my doctorate –

HOLLY. Harvard, right?

DR. MCNUTHIN. California State is every bit as good.

HOLLY. Whatever gets you through the night.

DR. MCNUTHIN. *(Sharp)* Spoiled children make bad parents.

***DR. MCNUTHIN** is a lap dummy that is a fully-manipulated puppet *(thanks to some stage magic)* and looks exactly like Carol Channing. Believe me: These exist!

(pause)

HOLLY. I'm not that spoiled.

DR. MCNUTHIN. Compared to whom?

HOLLY. Demi Moore. She has a whole HOUSE for her dolls!

DR. MCNUTHIN. You're not Demi Moore.

HOLLY. Therefore, I'm not spoiled.

DR. MCNUTHIN. Just outta curiosity, when is the last time your father punished you?

HOLLY. *(stamping her foot)* He's doing it now! He won't let have that doll and he knows I *WANT* it!

DR. MCNUTHIN. Does he beat you? Has he ever grounded you? Put you in time out? The thinking chair? Anything???

*(**HOLLY** thinks, realizes **MCNUTHIN** has a point, which makes her angrier.)*

HOLLY. You are lousy at this!

DR. MCNUTHIN. I am not!

HOLLY. No. You're *abysmal*! You're supposed to tell me it's good that I'm expressing my feelings and that I'm entitled to them and that I'm always *right*!

DR. MCNUTHIN. This might be a good time to revisit the Anger Management training we began about a year ago. I thought you were making progress, but you've gotten steadily worse since church camp.

HOLLY. YOU'RE AN ASSWIPE!

DR. MCNUTHIN. HOLLY! Would Pastor Dave like you using that kind of language?

*(**HOLLY** smiles and gets dreamy.)*

HOLLY. Uh-uh.

DR. MCNUTHIN. And who likes Pastor Dave?

HOLLY. *I* like Pastor Dave.

Pastor Dave has the cutest dimples to ever land on cheeks.

DR. MCNUTHIN. Holly? Tell me, child. What is this new-found religion really about? What emptiness are you trying to fill?

HOLLY. That's it!

*(**HOLLY** grabs her and heads to the back area.)*

DR. MCNUTHIN. *What?*

HOLLY. I hate it when you try to make me cry.

DR. MCNUTHIN. Adoption!

(pause)

If you must pray to a fundamentalist god, at least consider giving the baby away. Think about all the parents who'd love a beautiful new baby. All the parents – *Christian* parents – that can't have one on their own.

HOLLY. It's a possibility.

Of course…isn't it harder, though? To get black babies adopted? Everybody wants little Aryan kids nowadays. Or baby girls from China. Not like in the 80s. No one wants Arnold, Willis or Webster now. What if no one wants my baby?

DR. MCNUTHIN. But your baby's *bi*-racial. That should improve its chances.

*(**HOLLY** becomes suddenly enraged.)*

HOLLY. That's enough!

*(**HOLLY** grabs **DR. MCNUTHIN**.)*

DR. MCNUTHIN. But – But – I just want to help –

HOLLY. You want to hurt!

DR. MCNUTHIN. You have to be honest with yourself!

HOLLY. One more word and your not going back in the box! You're not even goin' on E-bay! I'll put your ass on **Craig's List**!

DR. MCNUTHIN. You little tyrant!

HOLLY. SHUT UP!

(We hear a loud slam and then there's a pause. After a moment **HOLLY** *returns. She picks up her dust rag as if to go back to cleaning, but on second thought, she throws it down. After a moment:)*

BLACK DOLL 2. *(sings the first full line from the* Diff'rent Strokes *theme song*[*]*)*

NOW, THE WORLD DON'T MOVE TO THE BEAT OF JUST ONE DRUM

ALL BLACK DOLLS. *(sing the second full line from the* Diff'rent Strokes *theme song*[**]*)*

HOLLY. *(sings)*

THE MAN IS BALD –

ALL BLACK DOLLS. WHAT?!

BLACK DOLL 2. I know *that* ain't the lyric.

HOLLY. I like it that way. And Mr. Drummond *was* bald!

BLACK DOLL 2. It's wrong.

HOLLY. Now that I have Jesus, I'm never wrong.

---

*Please see Music Use Note on page 3

**Please see Music Use Note on page 3

Scene Three

(Late at night. **HOLLY** *is playing a video game. We see her maneuvering a control pad while facing out. Lights flickering on her face should indicate the TV screen. There is a light knock at the window on the back wall, but we can't see who is there.* **HOLLY** *quickly and quietly turns off the TV and ducks low so that she is hidden by the couch. The person at the window knocks again louder, then tries to open the window. When this doesn't work, the visitor bangs on the window once again before leaving. There is a silence for a few moments. Then* **HOLLY** *slowly rises, turns the TV and video game back on and begins to play again.)*

HOLLY. *(smug)* Neanderthal.

Scene Four

(**HOLLY** *and* **MIA** *sit at the table.* **MIA** *is reading a book and* **HOLLY** *is taking a test.* **MIA** *glances at her watch.)*

MIA. Two minutes.

(**HOLLY** *glares at* **MIA**, *but scribbles on her paper quickly. We wait. Finally,* **HOLLY** *slams her pencil down on the table.)*

HOLLY. Done. With time to spare, I bet.

MIA. Great.

(**MIA** *takes* **HOLLY**'*s paper and places it in a folder and then puts the folder in her bag.)*

HOLLY. Aren't you gonna grade it?

MIA. I will at home tonight.

HOLLY. Do it now.

MIA. We have other things to do right now.

HOLLY. But I want to see the pleasure you get from my responses. They're accurate as well as humorous.

MIA. It's Trig.

HOLLY. Read between the vectors.

MIA. I'll give you the full report on Monday.

(pause)

HOLLY. Fine.

Hungry. Go get my lunch. And some CapriSuns. Three of 'em.

MIA. It's only 10:30.

HOLLY. How many children have *you* carried in your womb?

(**MIA** *starts up the stairs.)*

Yep. That's what I thought.

MIA. *(mumbling)* I should get paid extra for this.

HOLLY. Take it up with your Union Rep.

(**MIA** *exits.)*

JAPANESE TEA SERVER. Holly?

HOLLY. Yes, my darling?

JAPANESE TEA SERVER. You know how much I adore your company, don't you?

HOLLY. The feeling is mutual.

JAPANESE TEA SERVER. So I hope you do not misinterpret my meaning by asking you about that Japanese Wagasa Geisha…

(pause)

Your father – that kind and *handsome* man – brought her here in a bag. Did he not?

HOLLY. What're you gettin' at?

JAPANESE TEA SERVER. I would so love to have her standing beside me. We would make your collection one to be envied! Even by the doll enthusiasts in South Dakota! Think of it, Holly! We could get your profile in *Dolls Monthly*. We could get you on the local news! We could get you on *FOX*!

HOLLY. That would be very nice but he told me no. I can't have her. As I'm sure you heard.

JAPANESE TEA SERVER. No. I heard him say "yes." Only you have to compromise.

HOLLY. You want me to get an abortion so you can hang out with a *Geisha*?!

JAPANESE TEA SERVER. SHE'S MY SISTER!

HOLLY. That's enough now.

JAPANESE TEA SERVER. Oh, come on! Don't you want to be a *star*?!

HOLLY. Fame is temporary. Faith is forever.

JAPANESE TEA SERVER. You said you love me! Have a heart!

(The basement door opens.)

HOLLY. As you were!

*(***JAPANESE TEA SERVER** *shuts up.* **MIA** *enters carrying a tray with a sandwich, a salad, an apple, and three CapriSun drinks. She places it on the table beside*

HOLLY'*s work.* **MIA** *sits and watches as* **HOLLY** *begins to eat.)*

MIA. You're welcome by the way.

HOLLY. *(while stuffing her face)* Thanks.

*(***MIA** *looks around.)*

MIA. There are so many…eyes. In this room.

HOLLY. At last count: 472.

MIA. Seriously?

HOLLY. 236 pairs.

MIA. I'll be honest: they kinda scare me. I had a nightmare last night that I was strapped to a bed in a hospital maternity ward and all the nurses, babies, and doctors were all dolls. Creepy dolls. *Talking* dolls.

(pause)

But it's a little inappropriate for me to tell you about my dreams, I guess.

HOLLY. Very.

MIA. You talk to your dolls, don't you?

(Pause; **HOLLY** *eyes her suspiciously for a moment. Then continues eating.)*

HOLLY. Don't even try it. We're not that close.

MIA. No I s'pose not. What about people who *are* close to you? What do your friends think a this – collection?

*(***HOLLY** *shrugs.)*

HOLLY. So? You work out?

MIA. Little kickboxing.

HOLLY. Shut up no way!

MIA. Gimme an assailant. I'll prove it.

HOLLY. Wow! Can you teach me?

MIA. Not sure how safe it is for pregnant girls to start kickboxing. I think they usually do yoga.

HOLLY. *(disappointed)* Boring.

You have boyfriend?

MIA. Sort of.

HOLLY. Are you a lesbian?

MIA. No.

HOLLY. Bi?

MIA. No! Why would you ask that?

HOLLY. "Sort of" is vague. So I thought you were covering up something interesting. Or sinful. You don't have to talk to me about this stuff. Since it makes you so nervous.

MIA. Yes, I have a boyfriend. But we are having some problems right now. Does that satisfy your curiosity?

HOLLY. What kind of problems?

*(**MIA** sighs and begins to go through papers.)*

MIA. We have some cultural differences that we're trying to overcome.

HOLLY. What culture?

MIA. He's Somalian.

HOLLY. From Africa, right?

MIA. That's where Somalia is.

HOLLY. So what? He wants like a bunch of wives or somethin'? That sucks.

MIA. Eat your lunch.

HOLLY. C'mon tell me!

MIA. He wants to get married and start having babies and I don't.

(pause)

HOLLY. That doesn't sound cultural.

MIA. Well, it is.

HOLLY. Maybe you're just uptight.

*(**MIA** stares at her.)*

MIA. OK, Spectra, what about *your* boyfriend?

HOLLY. I don't have a boyfriend.

*(**HOLLY** keeps eating. **MIA** stares at her.)*

MIA. So, how exactly did you – I mean, who's the – um – ya know . . .

HOLLY. What's he look like?

MIA. Who?

HOLLY. Your boyfriend! You have a picture of him?

MIA. Oh. No. I see him enough as it is.

HOLLY. Here's my tray.

*(***HOLLY** *hands it to her.* **MIA** *starts back upstairs.)*

Leave the door open.

*(***MIA** *exits, leaving the door open.)*

HOLLY. *(Yelling up the stairs:)* Here's the real question: Does he have any pictures of *you*?

*(***MIA** *returns and closes the door.)*

MIA. Yeah. He has a digital camera his sponsor gave him last Christmas. He – He has one on his computer at his job.

HOLLY. Sounds like you guys are in two different relationships.

MIA. You're quite level-headed. At your core, I mean.

HOLLY. Thank you.

MIA. I find it surprising sometimes. That you're pregnant. Incongruent.

HOLLY. *(quietly)* Me too.

(a pause)

MIA. Do you wonder what it looks like? Right now?

HOLLY. What?

MIA. The - fetus. Do you ever picture it?

HOLLY. I don't know.

Do you ever think about reincarnation?

MIA. Not often. Why?

(The dolls giggle mischievously. **HOLLY** *glares at them.)*

HOLLY. Never mind. We have work to do.

(**MIA** *stares at* **HOLLY**.)

MIA. *(referring to* **HOLLY**'*s stomach)* How did it happen?

(Pause; **HOLLY** *leans in very close to* **MIA**. **MIA** *is very interested.)*

HOLLY. The sperm…found the egg. It was a miracle.

(**HOLLY** *sits with her notebook open and a pen in her hand, ready to take notes.)*

Meter's running. I'd like to be educated.
If you don't mind.

(**MIA** *just stares at* **HOLLY**.)

Scene Five

(Late at night. **HOLLY** *is trying to sleep, but is distressed and can't lay still. Finally she gets up and grabs several dolls from the various shelves and places them on the floor in an arc and then sits with them.)*

HOLLY. I know it's late, but this is important. It requires a solid resolution. Mr. Secretary General.

(She speaks to an African Male Doll, who will be **KOFI ANNAN.***)*

KOFI. I think I know what Holly needs us to decide. Is there any opposition to the adoption question at present? China? Any thoughts?

JAPANESE TEA SERVER. Abortion! Abortion! I want my sister back!

KOFI. I said *China*! What about you, Russia?

(A Russian Babushka doll speaks in a thick Russian accent.)

RUSSIAN DOLL. Nyet! Adoption is best for all. And Holly can take part in process by screening potential parents.

HOLLY. I can?

KOFI. India?

AMERICAN-INDIAN DOLL. First of all I am offended to the point of vomiting that you just called me *India*! You motherfuckers are the reason why the American Indian Movement in this country is either dead, drunk, or incarcerated!

KOFI. Thank you for staying on topic! Iran?

IRANIAN MALE DOLL. Yes! There are no homosexuals in Iran. (That's all I'm at liberty to say right now.)

KOFI. *(to* **HOLLY***)* This is a tough one, my dear. I don't think we can pass a resolution tonight.

HOLLY. Yeah. I figured it was asking too much, but I thought it couldn't hurt to –

(Suddenly the visitor is back and uses a crowbar to pry the window open.)

KOFI. Maybe you should get *his* opinion.

*(**HOLLY** watches as **YAGER** crawls through the window and falls to the floor. He picks himself up and casually brushes himself off.)*

YAGER. 'Sup, Holly?

HOLLY. You're not supposed to be in here.

YAGER. I know but I found a key!

(He holds up the crowbar, laughing.)

HOLLY. Maybe I didn't *want* you to find a key!

*(**YAGER** belches at **HOLLY**.)*

HOLLY. *Gross*! I'm callin' the cops! This is breaking and entering and you're going to jail!

*(**YAGER** blocks the stairs so **HOLLY** can't exit.)*

YAGER. *(impersonating **HOLLY**'s father)* Relax, Holly Bear! Looky: I got you Pop Rocks!

*(**YAGER** gives **HOLLY** a packet. She reluctantly sits on the couch.)*

Remember that story about that kid that ate the Pop Rocks and a can a Pepsi at the same time and then his head exploded? Tonight's the night. I'm goin' for this shit!

*(**YAGER** pours two packets of Pop Rocks into his mouth and then he takes a can of Pepsi from his pocket and swallows nearly the whole can. **HOLLY** watches him. They wait for several seconds. He shakes his head violently like a puppy who's just had a bath.)*

YAGER. Wow. That was a let down.

HOLLY. Tell me about it.

*(**HOLLY** eats the Pop Rocks. **YAGER** stares at her.)*

YAGER. Ain't seen you in awhile.

HOLLY. That wasn't an accident.

YAGER. Where you been at?

HOLLY. *(sighs)* The correct way to ask that question is: Where have you been? Not: "Where you been at!"

YAGER. Thought maybe you were dead.

HOLLY. I wasn't.

YAGER. Nope. Jus' livin' in a big-ass tomb.

HOLLY. I like it here. Best place there is.

YAGER. The biggest doll finally moves in. That's…what's the word? Ironic.

HOLLY. You're an idiot. There's nothing ironic about it. If anything it's symbolic, but I wouldn't even say that.

YAGER. Still straight A's, huh?

HOLLY. *(mocking his voice)* Still illiterate, huh?

YAGER. Not anymore.

I know what ironic means.

HOLLY. Doubt it.

YAGER. Can I play *Tomb Raider*?

HOLLY. No! It's mine! And that's a sinful game. I don't play that now.

YAGER. You sound like a nun!

HOLLY. Don't like it? Get out!

*(**YAGER** knocks a few dolls out of the way and begins thumbing through her video games.)*

YAGER. Super Noah's Ark 2? What the Hell is this?

HOLLY. It's a Christian game! It was a gift!

YAGER. Is it fun?

*(**HOLLY** considers.)*

HOLLY. No.

YAGER. I want Lara Croft.

*(**YAGER** continues going through her games.)*

How was church camp? Did you sing and testify and baptize cats and shit?

HOLLY. You wouldn't understand because you're too hopelessly ignorant, but church camp changed my life. I accepted Jesus Christ into my heart and since then, everything has been different. Maybe *you* should've gone. Seems to me you need some Christian guidance more than I ever did, but again: your natural ignorance and cultivated stupidity prevent the necessary self-reflection involved.

YAGER. *(Finds the game and puts it in the console as he speaks.)* You're a really bitchy Christian.

HOLLY. Instead of letting you know what I really think of you, I'm just going to pray. For your soul.

YAGER. Cool.

*(**YAGER** plays the game. **HOLLY** begins to pick up her dolls. Before she can get to it, **YAGER** snatches the **JAPANESE TEA SERVER**.)*

YAGER. Leave her out. I always thought she was kinda hot. I might have to kidnap her.

*(He laughs; **HOLLY** fumes, but calmly puts the other dolls away.)*

HOLLY. Something tells me you won't figure this out for yourself so I guess I have to say it: Things aren't going to be like they were before.

YAGER. Oh yeah? You mean like tryin' to lock me out? 'Cuz that was new.

HOLLY. You can't come here anymore.

*(**YAGER** loses the game and we can audibly hear this somehow. He looks at **HOLLY**.)*

YAGER. Why not?

HOLLY. Because I don't want you here!

(He stands and regards her.)

YAGER. Awww. Somebody's grumpy today. I think *I* know what Holly Bear wants!

HOLLY. No, don't!

YAGER. I know what she wants!

HOLLY. Stop it! It's not funny!

YAGER. Holly Bear wants the big, bad, Tickle Bear!

*(***YAGER*** grabs her and throws her on the couch, tickling the Hell out of her.* **HOLLY** *laughs uncontrollably.)*

HOLLY. *(while laughing)* I hate you! I hate you so much!

YAGER. Yes! Yes! She hates the Tickle Bear as much as she LOVES him!

HOLLY. *(still laughing)* No I really *hate* you!

(Suddenly **YAGER** *begins kissing* **HOLLY**. *This becomes intense fast. At first,* **HOLLY** *lets him and then suddenly as if remembering something, she pushes him off and jumps up.)*

(no longer laughing) No way, man.

*(***YAGER*** is confused.)*

YAGER. Thought we were having fun.

*(***YAGER*** picks up the* **JAPANESE TEA SERVER** *and caresses her hair, rather tenderly.)*

So that's it? You find Jesus and we're just – we're not gonna do it anymore?

*(***HOLLY*** shakes her head. Pause.)*

Well. That kinda blows.

(He opens another packet of Pop Rocks and throws it in his mouth. As he does this, **HOLLY** *cautiously takes* **JAPANESE TEA SERVER** *from him and puts her away.)*

HOLLY. Yager. You have to go home now.

YAGER. I don't know why but I get the distinct feeling that you're keepin' some like huge secret from me.

HOLLY. Nope.

YAGER. Like some enormous big, *fat* secret that relates to me somehow. Wait a minute…are you seeing some Christian Bible guy? Some like Kirk Cameron fuckin' *Left Behind* guy?

HOLLY. No and it's none of your business anyway!

YAGER. Do you need another visit from the tickle bear?

HOLLY. I'm gettin' my Dad and you will NOT be happy to see him.

YAGER. *(alarmed)* Oh OK. I'll leave. I'm leaving.

*(**YAGER** grabs his crowbar and clumsily climbs back out of the window. He gets to the other side and reaches in, trying to touch her.)*

Is everything OK?

HOLLY. I told you. Everything's better now.

YAGER. No. You said different.

HOLLY. I meant better.

YAGER. You still love me, nerd?

*(**HOLLY** quickly pulls the window down and **YAGER** whips his hand out just in time. **YAGER** stares; he's still confused. He peers through the window so long that **HOLLY** finally closes the curtain.)*

Scene Six - Second trimester

*(**HOLLY** and **MIA** are working.)*

MIA. C'mon focus. What major body of water lies next to Kenya?

HOLLY. The Indian Ocean.

DAD. *(enters as if in the midst of an argument)* You have to go! There is no argument you can make that will change my mind! You're going into the fourth month –

MIA. When is Kenya's Independence Day?

HOLLY. December 12th, 1965.

MIA. Wrong.

HOLLY. Excuse me?

DAD. Do you hear me talking to you? What if there are… complications? You have to see a doctor!

MIA. I said: Wrong. Try again.

DAD. *(kindly, to **MIA**:)* I'm sorry to interrupt. You are doing such a wonderful job with Holly –

MIA. Thank you.

DAD. I just need a moment to talk to her or she won't –

HOLLY. Negative! You're disrupting my education! Which is rather costly, isn't it?

DAD. Goddammit, Holly!

MIA. Fine.

*(**MIA** steps to the side.)*

HOLLY. Stop saying "Goddammit" and "Jesus Christ!" *Please*!

DAD. I have never laid a hand on you, but you are tempting fate, little one!

HOLLY. You're gonna beat me in front of my tutor? Beat me *and* my unborn child?

DAD. You are gonna leave this basement and get an ultrasound if I have to carry you out gagged, blindfolded, and hog-tied in a Hefty bag!

(pause)

DAD. *(cont.)* I was being figurative.

MIA. Can I say something?

*(**DAD** shrugs like: "Why not?")*

Holly? Why don't you want to go to the doctor?

HOLLY. You all know full well that I cannot leave my religious exile until this baby pops out. I've made this abundantly clear.

MIA. What if something's wrong with the baby?

HOLLY. If something is wrong, there's nothing a doctor can do about it. The only answers will come through prayer.

DAD. Oh, Jesus H. Christ.

*(**HOLLY** is about to rage when:)*

MIA. What if – and this is a big if, but just answer hypothetically – what if the doctor…came to you?

(pause)

You wouldn't have to leave and you could make sure the baby and you are healthy and on the right track. Would that be fair?

DAD. How the Hell am I supposed to –

*(**MIA** gently puts a hand out to shut **DAD** up.)*

HOLLY. I guess that would be OK.

MIA. *(just to **DAD**)* My aunt's an OB/GYN. Never hurts to ask.

DAD. *(surprised)* OK. Thank you. But – I – I worry about making *every*thing easy for her.

MIA. Really?

DAD. *(just to **MIA**)* I imagine it doesn't look that way. But when I have to, I will put my foot down. Just yesterday she asked me for a *credit card*! You know what I told her?

*(**MIA** waits.)*

(proud) We'll see.

MIA. That's…great.

(Whisper:) I can't promise anything and I certainly don't want to enable her, but this might be one case where giving in is necessary.

DAD. *(Unconvinced that this will work; to* **HOLLY***:)* This is NOT over, Bubble!

*(***DAD** *exits.)*

HOLLY. Wow. He listens to you.

MIA. He certainly listens to *you.* If he didn't, I wouldn't be here. C'mon: Kenyan Independence Day.

*(***HOLLY** *thinks.)*

HOLLY. I told you: December 12th, 19 – oh. 1963. What do you mean you wouldn't be here?

(pause)

MIA. You know what I'm talking about.

*(***HOLLY** *stares at her blankly.)*

You run things around here. You are the topdog. Believe me: Daddy knows it.

HOLLY. Don't call him Daddy.

MIA. Next question: approximately how many refugees did Kenya host by the end of 2001?

HOLLY. Why are you obsessed with Africa?

MIA. *Some*body should be!

HOLLY. What for?

MIA. Sue me for trying to widen your scope of knowledge!

HOLLY. Maybe I will!

MIA. GOOD! You do that!

HOLLY. MAYBE I WILL!

MIA. GOOD! I HOPE YOU DO!

HOLLY. Good! 'Cuz I probably will!

MIA. Bring it on!

HOLLY. You're obnoxious.

MIA. You're just noxious

HOLLY. You're an Oreo!

(silence)

MIA. Why would you say something like that?

*(**HOLLY** shrugs.)*

HOLLY. They call me that, too. So whatever? I just started taking it as a compliment.

MIA. Do you think you're an Oreo?

HOLLY. No. I think I'm a Thin Mint.

MIA. I don't know what that means, but you do so why let the dicks of the world get under your skin?

HOLLY. I don't.

MIA. Seriously.

HOLLY. *(Really listening to her:)* OK.

MIA. Good. So. Refugees?

HOLLY. I don't want to talk about some smelly refugees.

MIA. You go from victim to predator faster than the speed of light in a vacuum.

HOLLY. Tachyons are faster.

MIA. Is there anything you *don't* know?

HOLLY. Hey! I just figured out what you're doing. You're lazy and you're trying to combine my schoolwork with your thesis research.

*(Pause. **MIA** glares at her.)*

I'm right, aren't I?

(teasing chant:) I'm smarter than you are! I'm smarter than you are!

Pretty soon I'll be able to read all your thoughts!

MIA. No. N-no. I refuse to allow you to transform me into a bratty sister. I don't even *have* a sister. I refuse to stoop any further.

HOLLY. That'd be hard for you, anyway. You're starting to get a little lumpy around the middle. South Beach not working out so well, huh?

MIA. Holly, we have work to do.

(Pause. Suddenly it seems **HOLLY** *might cry.)*

HOLLY. You're not fat! I'm projecting! It's me! I'm the fat one! I can't believe how much weight I've gained and I just can't stop eating and nobody cares!

MIA. And you've gained what? Ten pounds? Twelve? That's normal. Nothing to be ashamed of.

HOLLY. I wish I could be so scientific about it. But I can't. Not when I look like a moose!

MIA. Actually that's a misconception. Moose are large, but typically not overweight. They tend to be athletic animals.

HOLLY. *(Dry:)* Thank you.

MIA. Are we moving on or having a hormonal meltdown? Either is fine, but tell me now so I can prepare.

HOLLY. Moving on.

*(***HOLLY** *gets up and starts cleaning the doll shelves.)*

MIA. If I can get my aunt to bring her equipment down here, will you cooperate with her? Let her examine you?

HOLLY. Whatever.

MIA. No! It's not "whatever," Holly. If I'm going to ask –

HOLLY. Yes.

(pause)

MIA. Fine. I'll see what I can do.

HOLLY. 220,000 refugees.

MIA. That's right.

HOLLY. Was your boyfriend one of 'em?

(pause)

MIA. Adroit.

Yes. He was.

HOLLY. Bet that sucked. Is that what your obsession is about?

(**MIA** *shrugs.)*

MIA. Maybe we've done enough of this for the day. Where are you on your Sister Aimee Semple McPherson term paper?

HOLLY. I need a plate with a large amount of French Fries and ketchup now.

MIA. Holly . . .

HOLLY. Right now. Then after that, we can go back to whatever you want. OK?

(**MIA** *stares at her.)*

MIA. We're gonna have to figure out a way to curtail your cravings because this is getting ridiculous!

HOLLY. Yeah. Good luck with that. Don't forget the salt.

(**MIA** *stomps up the stairs.)*

DR. MCNUTHIN. *(off stage)* Holly?

HOLLY. Yeah. All right.

(**HOLLY** *exits and returns carrying* **DR. MCNUTHIN**. *She places her in her chair.)*

DR. MCNUTHIN. Glasses please?

(**HOLLY** *looks around. She looks for a while. She can't find them.)*

HOLLY. I can't find them anywhere.

DR. MCNUTHIN. Fuck me!

HOLLY. Well, maybe you should just wear them all the time and this wouldn't happen!

DR. MCNUTHIN. I don't need them all the time.

HOLLY. I don't know what to tell you.

DR. MCNUTHIN. Are you tryin' to fuck with me? 'Cuz I will NOT be fucked with!

HOLLY. I DIDN'T DO IT!

(**DR. MCNUTHIN** *sighs.)*

DR. MCNUTHIN. Since I can't fucking see, I'm going to keep this brief and then you can put me the fuck back: Do everything the girl upstairs says.

HOLLY. God! I –

(**HOLLY** *catches herself.*)

HOLLY. Excuse me.

I mean – Geez, I already said I would! She's gonna get some crazy witch doctor to come and see me. I said I'd cooperate, didn't I? She wants me to work like Einstein even though

(ylling at the ceiling:) I'm PREGNANT and I'm TIRED and I'm HUNGRY! But I said I'd do it! What is the big deal?

DR. MCNUTHIN. The big deal is you can write me off pretty easily if you want. Just label me a psychological projection from your head, which would be a pedestrian way to view our relationship, but that would pretty much shut me the fuck up for good. But you can't dismiss girlfriend upstairs so easily. You gotta listen to her. Even if it pisses you off and you start to – you know – hate her.

HOLLY. We're not exactly "BFFs" right now.

DR. MCNUTHIN. That may deteriorate.

HOLLY. I don't see how that's even possible.

DR. MCNUTHIN. Well you been warned. I'm getting a fucking migraine put me back.

HOLLY. What are you a soothsayer, now? That's not your function!

DR. MCNUTHIN. I can't do my fucking function without my fucking glasses!

(**DR. MCNUTHIN** *holds back tears.*)

Find them. And you can have a psychotherapist again. Until then, I'm no better than Cassandra at the fucking House of Atreus.

(**HOLLY** *looks around again. She finds the glasses and places them on* **DR. MCNUTHIN***'s face.* **DR. MCNUTHIN***'s demeanor changes completely.)*

DR. MCNUTHIN. Ah. That's so much better. Well, honey, I think that's all the time we have for today.

HOLLY. *What?*

DR. MCNUTHIN. But I feel I've made my point quite clear.

(Basement door opens and **MIA** *enters with a plate of French Fries and ketchup. She sits them down.)*

MIA. *(She jumps when she sees* **DR. MCNUTHIN.***)* Oh my G–! That is the creepiest doll!

HOLLY. *(eating ravenously)* That's subjective. Where's the salt?

MIA. I pre-salted them.

HOLLY. You're lying.

MIA. You have too much sodium in your diet.

HOLLY. They have no taste!

MIA. Wait a minute!

(**MIA** *stares at* **DR. MCNUTHIN.***)*

She looks like Carol Channing!

(**HOLLY** *glares at* **MIA.***)*

You don't know who that is, do you?

(**HOLLY** *shakes her head.)*

MIA. She was a legend of Broadway. She was in *Hello, Dolly*!

(**MIA** *sings the last 5 lines of "Before the Parade Passes By" from* Hello, Dolly! *Doing her best Channing impression, which isn't great."*)*

I'M GONNA RAISE THE ROOF…

I was in that show. I was Ermengarde. I didn't have a song.

HOLLY. Sorry. I don't know music from the 40s.

---

*Please see Music Use Note on page 3

MIA. Does *your* Carol Channing sing?

HOLLY. I know what you're up to.

MIA. What am I up to?

HOLLY. Yes. Sometimes I communicate with my dolls. And yes. They sometimes communicate back. There. Happy? I hope this amuses you to no end. I hope you have a good laugh later with your refugee boyfriend!

MIA. Oh *shit*! Tomorrow's his birthday.

*(**MIA** grabs her appointment book and writes something down quickly. Or it can be an iPhone. Whatever.)*

He is the hardest, hardest person to buy gifts for. He pretends he likes *every*thing, but he doesn't.

HOLLY. I'm easy. If I could have anything I wanted for my birthday, it'd be a Monika. But I never asked Dad. They're just too expensive.

MIA. Not *another* doll?

HOLLY. Not any doll. Monika's a German artist. Her dolls are beautiful works of art. They look like real women. Fabulous women on their way to some fancy dress-up ball. But it's their faces that are special. Sometimes they look pensive or like they're hiding something. They don't smile.

But. They're expensive. Usually they go for 15 or 16.

MIA. *Hundred?*

HOLLY. Sure. Which is nothing for serious collectors.

MIA. Insane.

HOLLY. Do – did you have dolls?

MIA. I used to have some. But I wasn't like you. I'd take 'em apart, exchange their limbs and other body parts like I was Dr. Frankenstein. Eventually, my mom said "No more dolls! You're too destructive!" I actually tried to make one once. Stitched her body together, used stuffing from an old pillow and gave her a Styrofoam head that I drew on with magic markers. Called her Junior. Sometimes I pulled her in my wagon and played crazy eights with her. I always won. Who knows? Maybe I coulda been like Monika the German artist.

HOLLY. Do you still have it?

MIA. No. My dog got ahold of her one night – I don't wanna talk about that.

HOLLY. You were an only child. Like me.

MIA. T.M.I. We really need to get back on track.

HOLLY. Have *you* ever been pregnant?

(pause)

MIA. Time to get back to work.

HOLLY. I've been ready and waitin'. You're the one talkin' about your homemade friend.

DR. MCNUTHIN. You're gonna have to try harder than this.

*(**MIA** suddenly glances at **DR. MCNUTHIN**.)*

MIA. Did – ?

HOLLY. What?

MIA. Sometimes – this basement gets a little spooky. Sometimes.

HOLLY. I've never noticed that.

MIA. Fine. Let's uh – Yes. Sister Aimee. What do you have so far?

DR. MCNUTHIN. *(closed jaw whisper)* Better watch her. She's a little sharper than I thought.

Scene Seven

(Later. Nighttime. **HOLLY** *types on a computer. She pauses to think. She comes to an answer.)*

HOLLY. *(as she types it)* Sister Aimee Semple McPherson: Why the Best People are Always Misunderstood.

(She thinks about her title.)

Yeah. That's brilliant.

WHITE DOLL. You don't even want a baby.

HOLLY. Shhh! I'm working.

JAPANESE TEA SERVER. Oh, be nice to her. Holly, what she means is you don't *need* a baby. Subtle, but there's a difference.

HOLLY. Maybe I do want one.

WHITE DOLL. Bullshit!

BLACK DOLL 2. You lie like a relaxer.

HOLLY. Zip it. I'm busy.

*(***HOLLY** *goes back to typing.)*

RUSSIAN DOLL. *(in Russian)* She is not listening to us.

HOLLY. What?

JAPANESE TEA SERVER. *(in Japanese)* Yeah. We may have to take drastic measures.

HOLLY. *(frightened:)* What are you doing?

WHITE DOLL. *(in Danish)* This is exciting! *(Det er spændende.)*

HOLLY. Stop it!

(All the foreign dolls begin to speak at once in a hyper cacophony of languages **HOLLY** *cannot understand. As they reach a crescendo:)*

HOLLY. STOP IT STOP IT STOP IT!!

DR. MCNUTHIN. *(off stage) You* stop it! Quit panicking and come get me.

(All the lights go out and the dolls laugh, mischievously. **HOLLY** *screams.)*

HOLLY. What are you trying to do to me?!

JAPANESE TEA SERVER. Holly, we don't mean to scare you, but…you can't have a baby. We simply cannot allow it.

DR. MCNUTHIN. *(off stage)* Have you all lost your minds?

BLACK DOLL 2. Consider this a friendly warning. Holly Bear.

(footsteps from above)

DAD. *(calling from upstairs)* Holly?

(The lights come back on. The dolls are now surrounding **HOLLY**.*)*

(off stage) Why was it so dark down there? What's going on?

RUSSIAN DOLL. Tell him everything is fine. And it will be.

HOLLY. *(Afraid:)* Everything is fine, Dad.

DAD. *(off stage)* I'm coming down.

HOLLY. No! Don't. I just had a nightmare. That's all.

(beat)

DAD. *(off stage)* Something feels odd.

HOLLY. No. I'm fine. It was a – a pregnancy nightmare. Hormones. 'Night, Dad.

DAD. *(off stage)* Oh. All right.

(pause)

HOLLY. Take me to your leader.

(The dolls laugh hysterically.)

JAPANESE TEA SERVER. What a silly request.

RUSSIAN DOLL. You are the one with the power.

WHITE DOLL. Use it.

HOLLY. You little ingrates! I treat you with nothing but kindness and this is how you repay me?!

ALL DOLLS. Are you certain you understand the meaning of the word "kindness?" Are you confused or intentionally being deceitful?

HOLLY. Neither!

WHITE DOLL. We've been patient with you.

QUEEN VICTORIA. Some might say…indulgent.

JAPANESE TEA SERVER. But our time is running out. We cannot have it, Holly.

ALL DOLLS. No babies. Never.

(**HOLLY** *picks up* **JAPANESE TEA SERVER** *and stares at her.*)

HOLLY. It wouldn't change anything.

JAPANESE TEA SERVER. You have all the power. You are the real leader here.

You certainly don't need an heir. Or heiress. Now do you?

(**HOLLY** *considers this.*)

Scene Eight

(In an anteroom in the back, we can hear beeping sounds and maybe see a strange light blinking through a semi-closed door and hear the murmur of voices.)

HOLLY. *(off stage)* Is it gonna hurt?

DOCTOR. *(off stage)* Just lie still. It'll be over soon.

(There is silence while we watch the empty stage. Silence. For a long time. Then:)

DR. MCNUTHIN. *(With cigarette in hand; not wearing her glasses:)* Any a you rug-munches got a light?

JAPANESE TEA SERVER. I'm sorry. I'd answer you, but the rules of Holly's caste system are finite.

DR. MCNUTHIN. Lick me, Madame Butterfly.

BLACK DOLL 2. Didn't you have a mastectomy?

DR. MCNUTHIN. That was Olivia Newton-John! For fuck's sake! Did I ask for a prognosis? No! I asked for a goddamned light?

QUEEN VICTORIA. You know, I usually do not speak on these matters as I prefer to reserve my rather chronologically advanced faculties for higher pursuits, but perhaps you should consider another outlet for your oral fixation. One that doesn't put us all at dire risk.

DR. MCNUTHIN. A simple yes or no will do.

ALL DOLLS. NO!

BLACK DOLL 2. Lemme translate Queenie's British English into normal English: We are *flammable*!

DR. MCNUTHIN. I know I know I *know*! I just needed a little stress reliever. Between the kid and you all plottin' like you're fuckin' COINTELPRO, my nerves are shot to shit.

BLACK DOLL. If you know what's good for ya, you will join us.

WHITE DOLL. Then you won't need a smoke.

JAPANESE TEA SERVER. Yes. Join us. United we stand. Isn't that what the white people say?

DR. MCNUTHIN. I ain't drinkin' the Kool-Aid, Reverend Jones.

JAPANESE TEA SERVER. You think you're safe? She'll forget all about you, too.

DR. MCNUTHIN. Maybe it's for the best. Jesus, I'm sick of life at the kiddie table!

BLACK DOLL 2. Careful what you wish for.

JAPANESE TEA SERVER. I don't see your problem. Holly's young. Which is what she *should* be. Forever.

DR. MCNUTHIN. I'm gettin' sick a "young."

AMERICAN-INDIAN DOLL. Don't even get me started on that! That brat's so sheltered she thinks the whole world looks like us. Pretty, frozen, and powerless.

BLACK DOLL. Speak for yourself.

AMERICAN-INDIAN DOLL. Outta all of us, how come I am the ONLY representative from my tribe?

DR. MCNUTHIN. One a you is plenty!

JAPANESE TEA SERVER. You are all quarreling because you are afraid.

AMERICAN-INDIAN DOLL. *(to* **MCNUTHIN***)* Don't think you're above a beatdown just 'cuz you're the queen bitch around here.

QUEEN VICTORIA. I beg to differ.

DR. MCNUTHIN. Was that supposed to be a threat?

AMERICAN-INDIAN DOLL. I will whip your ass.

DR. MCNUTHIN. Then come on down outta that box, Sacajawea!

AMERICAN-INDIAN DOLL. No you did *not*!

BLACK DOLL 2. I'm takin' bets. Anyone?

KOFI ANNAN. Maybe we should try to resolve this by committee.

JAPANESE TEA SERVER. We must stay focused! Our lives are in peril and you *know* it!

DR. MCNUTHIN. Fuck that! What are you gonna do? *Scalp* me?

(Suddenly **AMERICAN-INDIAN DOLL***'s box falls off the shelf and on top of* **DR. MCNUTHIN. DR. MCNUTHIN** *screams.)*

AMERICAN-INDIAN DOLL. I WILL KILL YOU!

DR. MCNUTHIN. Ha! I'll beat you like you're Ethel Merman!

(They fight. Then suddenly there is a huge, audible gasp from everyone in the anteroom. The dolls go silent.)

HOLLY. *(squeals)* TWINS?!

ALL DOLLS. *Twins?*

(sounds of footsteps coming into the basement.)

JAPANESE TEA SERVER. You see?

BLACK DOLL 2. Two enemies. *Two.*

AMERICAN-INDIAN DOLL. We'll disappear for sure.

DR. MCNUTHIN. *(gently)* Don't worry. Bitch. As usual, I'll take care of everything.

AMERICAN-INDIAN DOLL. And if your methods don't work? Hag?

JAPANESE TEA SERVER. Just…wait.

Scene Nine

(After the ultrasound. **DAD** *and* **MIA** *are alone in the basement.)*

DAD. Thank you.

MIA. No big deal.

DAD. No. *Gigantic* deal! *I* couldn't have done that on my own.

MIA. I was glad to help.

*(***MIA** *gathers her belongings.* **DAD** *watches her.)*

DAD. Are you – are you still in school?

MIA. I'm working on my master's thesis. But you know this. You read my résumé. Right?

DAD. Huh? Oh, yes. Of course. The Curriculum Vitae. I read it. Twice. Remind me: What's your area of study?

MIA. Urban Planning. Well – sort of.

DAD. Oh yeah! How could I forget? Close to my field. Any questions that you might have, anything architecture-related, feel free to ask. Anytime.

(pause)

DAD. Then again I'm not a teacher. I probably couldn't tell you anything you couldn't find in a book. So. Nevermind. Scratch that off your list.

MIA. No. I appreciate it. If I have any questions, I'll ask.

DAD. Surprised you're not going into education. With all your talent and experience . . .

MIA. You didn't read my résumé! This is my first teaching job ever!

DAD. I did! I didn't commit it to memory, I'm sorry to say. I just think you really are a gifted tutor. God knows we need good city planners, but teachers are more valuable. I think.

MIA. I wouldn't be that good.

DAD. You sell yourself short.

MIA. One-on-one isn't so hard. But I have trouble speaking in front of big groups. And at the center, they gave me a huge packet and textbooks to follow. Most of what I teach Holly, I've only learned myself the day before. I don't know what I'm doing.

DAD. You're good at faking it then.

MIA. Yeah I'm good at faking things.

DAD. Damn good.

MIA. Uh – Mr. Brannigan –

DAD. Call me Weston.

MIA. I thought your name was Greg.

DAD. It is. But I like "Weston."

MIA. I like Mr. Brannigan.

DAD. I'm actually a PhD.

MIA. *Doctor* Brannigan, do you need anything else? I'm sort of running late.

DAD. Oh, No, No! Go on ahead. You've been more help than – well, you've gone way above and beyond the call of duty.

MIA. Thanks.

(She doesn't move.)

Always have been painfully, painfully shy. A painfully shy person that talks too much, if that makes sense. I say things, stupid things and I can't stop myself and the whole time I'm thinking "Shut up! Shut up, you fool!"

DAD. There's a wonderful course you can take down at the Y in public speaking. One of my colleagues used to teach it. I can ask him if –

*(**MIA** kisses **DAD** on the mouth. Silence.)*

MIA. Yeah. I'd love for you to ask him about the course. If he's still involved and it's not too much trouble.

DAD. N – N – No. No trouble at all. I'll find his card – -

MIA. Good!

DAD. I can look for it now.

MIA. No! I'll just – how about you give it to Holly? And then she can give it to me. Tomorrow.

DAD. OK.

(pause)

MIA. Have a nice evening.

*(**MIA** runs upstairs. A few moments pass. **MIA** reenters.)*

I apologize. That was not the appropriate thing to do.

DAD. Didn't bother me.

MIA. *(Fast, like all in one breath:)* I've never tutored before and I was just – It wasn't premeditated it's just that you're very attractive for a man your age and my boyfriend's been pressuring me to marry him and move back to Somalia, which is still in the midst of a pretty nasty civil war, but he thinks that's propaganda, but I think CIA air strikes should be enough to give one pause and he can't give me an orgasm even with his tongue and when you really get at the bones of our relationship I'm just not that attracted to him and we only became involved because I interviewed him for my thesis proposal which was originally about the urbanization and revitalization of war-torn villages in Eastern Africa and it seemed like the best way to understand the scope of the devastation was to fuck a lost boy.

(brief pause)

Only he's not Sudanese and he's not even that lost and my topic has evolved because I keep hearing about the scary cycle of teenage maternity in Africa, like did you know 40% of all babies born there are to girls under the age of *seventeen*? And this is a separate thing, but I have a huge problem with men. I often confuse any kind of strong feelings of respect or admiration for men with sexual attraction and then I just go ahead and have the sex and later I'm thinking "Why did I just do that" and then I tell myself "I don't know" and to shut myself up I just do it again so I thought if I were in a serious relationship that should stop it from happening and it's actually worked. To an extent and ultimately I think it all goes back to my father and our relationship was and is strained and he had this whole other family that lived on Archer Street and once when I was little I met my half-brother at Vacation Bible School and he said that Dad took him camping and to Minky's Farm and Petting Zoo. And I said "Really? He's never taken *me* to the corner to buy toilet paper." One time I told him I loved him and then I waited for him to say it back and he just nodded so I said "why don't you love me" and he said "love is a complicated construct and generally unnecessary."

(silence)

And also I had an abortion.

I have some problems. But nothing major.

(pause)

So you see? At this rate, I'll never finish my thesis.

DAD. *(As if he were Mike Brady:)* Well…if it'll help, you and I could fuck. But you realize it won't solve the conflict with your boyfriend. You have to be honest with him. It also won't solve the unhealthy attachments to men you seem to form, now would it?

MIA. I never thought of it like that. Thanks, Doctor Brannigan.

DAD. You're very welcome, dear.

HOLLY. *(from off)* Daddy?

*(**MIA** and **DAD** jump.)*

HOLLY. Are you there? Daddy?

MIA. *(whispers)* Night!

HOLLY. *(from off:)* Who are you talking to?

*(**MIA** runs upstairs and exits. Silence. **HOLLY** enters.)*

I don't feel good.

DAD. Hmm?

HOLLY. My stomach hurts.

DAD. You need your rest, Holly Bear.

(She sits next to him. He puts his arm around her.)

HOLLY. I dreamed about Mom.

DAD. Did you?

HOLLY. It was like the bad dreams I used to have where her death was all a mistake and she'd just gone into hiding and faked the whole thing. But this time she said she always knew I was God's favorite. And she said she started my doll collection so she could leave lots of women to look after me when she was gone. And they have. Wasn't that nice of her? And she knew it, Dad. She knew about the twins. She said the twins are for a purpose. One is my sacrifice. One is my **gift**. But then I woke up and she wasn't here anymore. And I felt sick and empty like usual. But everything she told me was true. See? I was right all along.

DAD. *(sighs)* Daddy loves you more than you can ever imagine. But he is really worried about his Bubble.

*(**HOLLY** becomes nauseous. She runs to the bathroom and vomits.)*

Scene Ten – Month 5

(**MIA** *is trying to teach* **HOLLY**, *but* **HOLLY** *is impossibly distracted.)*

MIA. We're really going to have to work on mechanics.

HOLLY. Like fixing cars?

MIA. Like writing sentences. You know what I mean. Punctuation is your friend!

(**HOLLY** *dumps a doll out of a basinet and begins fussing with it.)*

HOLLY. Don't worry. She's worthless. Three chips in her paint and she's missing a finger!

MIA. We don't have time to play.

HOLLY. I hope she's a girl. All my baby blankets are pink and purple or a combination of the two.

MIA. Holly, we're trying to work here.

HOLLY. I am working.

MIA. The PSATs are coming up soon. Remember? It's not just about math –

HOLLY. Yes it is. I can use my math skills to guess the odds. It's still multiple choice, right? That's elementary statistics. I'll be fine.

MIA. You can't just coast through.

HOLLY. Yellow. That's the color you're supposed to buy when you don't know the baby's sex.

MIA. Will you wake up?

(pause)

MIA. Leave the baby-doll clothes to the baby dolls. No one is gonna let you keep those babies.

HOLLY. Duh! That's why God gave me *twins*! One goes to the couple (Dad met the couple. He said they're cute. Episcopalians, but whatever) and the other one stays with me. Don't you understand anything? That's my gift for making the sacrifice!

MIA. What are you talking about? Are you from *Pluto*?

HOLLY. *(mumbling)* That's not really a planet.

MIA. Sacrifice?! You get three squares (sometimes six or seven) and you get to play with dolls all day long! You're incredibly intelligent, self-possessed, cocky as all Hell. Is this a nervous breakdown? I don't get it.

HOLLY. No. At church camp Pastor Dave said when we turn our lives over to Christ, He takes care of everything so we don't have to. I didn't believe him at first, either, but I like Pastor Dave. So I tried it. Turns out, he was right.

(pause)

And God will take care of my babies. *Both* of them. He knows they're special.

MIA. Did Pastor Dave know you were pregnant?

HOLLY. *I* didn't know it, yet. August 24th. That's the day I figured it out. August 24th. I got back from camp on August 22nd. But...Pastor Dave knew I sinned.

MIA. By having sex?

HOLLY. By letting it happen. I could've stopped it, but I didn't. I didn't try hard enough.

MIA. To stop it?

HOLLY. Can you order me some Buffalo wings?

MIA. Holly ...? Did you not *want* to have sex?

HOLLY. Not really. I used to – before I was saved – I sometimes...with my stupid neighbor. I don't even know why. It was so stupid.

MIA. Did he –

HOLLY. *(a simple fact)* I wasn't raped. If that's what you're asking. Is that what you're asking?

MIA. Yes.

HOLLY. No. We'd done it before. I just – I didn't really want to. Then. And I don't think he understood that. Or he thought I was kidding. Or...I don't know what he thought. But I let it happen. And Pastor Dave said I could wash that all away and I did and that's all I have to say about it and the number for Pepe's Pizza is 777-PEPE and I want twenty hot-n-spicy with Bleu cheese.

MIA. Holly…

HOLLY. Twenty hot-n-spicy with Bleu cheese!

MIA. You didn't sin.

HOLLY. You don't have the power –

MIA. You didn't.

(pause)

HOLLY. I wasn't raped. OK?

MIA. OK, Holly.

(pause)

HOLLY. Don't you pity me. OK?

MIA. OK, Holly.

You know? When you're older…you have plenty of time.

HOLLY. The baby's mine. She's half of a holy pair. Not just any baby. She's…The baby's mine. That's all.

MIA. Would that be best for her?

DR. MCNUTHIN. *(off stage)* You gotta listen, Holly.

HOLLY. 777-PEPE!! Or you're FIRED!

MIA. I'm dialing.

*(**MIA** picks up a cordless phone.)*

I'm sure God is sorry. I'm not anywhere near as special as God, but I'm sorry, too. And that's not pity. That's camaraderie. Woman to woman.

*(**MIA** dials the phone. **HOLLY** gently smiles.)*

Scene Eleven – Month 6

(The basement. **JAPANESE TEA SERVER** *is standing before a saucer and a cup of steaming tea. There are several new dolls strewn all over the room.)*

NEW DOLL. There's black and green mold in this basement. My pores will never survive this.

JAPANESE TEA SERVER. Get used to it. Mustiness is a part of your new life.

(Sound of a toilet flushing. **HOLLY** *eventually appears. She picks up a baby doll randomly.)*

BABY DOLL. What? What're you doing?

*(**HOLLY** begins to breast feed the doll.)*

HOLLY. I don't know what all the fuss is about. This isn't that hard.

BABY DOLL. That's because I'm not really able to suck.

HOLLY. Please stay in character.

*(**BABY DOLL** makes a perfect baby cry.)*

Awww.

(Singing lullaby-style; this should NOT sound soulful or melodic in any way:)

THE LORD SAID TO NOAH:
THERE'S GONNA BE A FLOODY, FLOODY
'LORD SAID TO NOAH:
THERE'S GONNA BE A FLOODY, FLOODY
GET THOSE CHILDREN OUT OF THE MUDDY, MUDDY
CHILDREN OF THE LORD

SO RISE AND SHINE
AND GIVE GOD YOUR GLORY, GLORY
RISE AND SHINE
AND GIVE GOD YOUR GLORY, GLORY
RISE AND SHINE AND –

JAPANESE TEA SERVER. Holly?

HOLLY. What do *you* want?

JAPANESE TEA SERVER. I made you a cup of tea.

*(***HOLLY** *stares at her. The dolls gather around.)*

We are sorry, Holly. We should be more understanding. Patient with you. We promise: no more tricks.

(The dolls make sounds of agreement. **HOLLY** *is moved.)*

HOLLY. I accept your apology.

*(***HOLLY** *picks up the cup of tea. As she's about to take a sip, a muffled scream is heard.)*

What was that?

JAPANESE TEA SERVER. The wind

BLACK DOLL 2. The rain

AMERICAN-INDIAN DOLL. 500 years of oppression

JAPANESE TEA SERVER. Drink. It's going to get cold.

(Another muffled scream. The dolls giggle, mischievously.)

HOLLY. What kind of tea is this?

JAPANESE TEA SERVER. Peppermint

BLACK DOLL 2. Chocolate

AMERICAN-INDIAN DOLL. Peyote

(Something strikes **HOLLY** *from behind and she jumps. She then sees* **DR. MCNUTHIN** *on the floor behind her.* **DR. MCNUTHIN** *is bound and gagged!)*

HOLLY. What have you monsters done?!

JAPANESE TEA SERVER. *(threatening)* Drink it, Holly! It's sweet. Like you.

*(***HOLLY** *uncovers* **DR. MCNUTHIN***'s mouth.)*

DR. MCNUTHIN. They'll die, Holly.

*(***HOLLY** *looks at the tea.)*

There's dandelion root in that tea.

JAPANESE TEA SERVER. Shut up! Holly, dandelions are healthy! They have vitamins and nutrients and –

DR. MCNUTHIN. You <u>will</u> miscarry. If you drink that tea.

*(**HOLLY** calmly takes the tea cup to the bathroom. We hear her pour it out. She returns.)*

JAPANESE TEA SERVER. Holly? She was lying to you! Trust me! You know how much I –

*(**HOLLY** rips **JAPANESE TEA SERVER**'s head off. She then discards the body. There is a deep silence. A murder has taken place. Beat. **HOLLY** disappears. The dolls are afraid.)*

BLACK DOLL 2. I can't believe it didn't work.

KOFI. I'm so ashamed.

*(**HOLLY** returns with a bottle of lighter fluid and a book of matches.)*

HOLLY. The insurrection ends now. Or would you like me to end it for you?

*(Silence. At the window, **YAGER** tries to again pry it open. It doesn't work. Suddenly **YAGER** smashes the window. Maybe some dolls scream. He climbs in. He's wearing a backpack.)*

YAGER. My "key" wasn't working.

HOLLY. How stupid can you be?

YAGER. I was just missin' ya.

HOLLY. But I don't miss *you*!

*(**YAGER** grabs her playfully and kisses her, but it's slightly threatening.)*

YAGER. You don't know what you miss.

(There is the sound of movement from upstairs.)

HOLLY. My Dad's coming! You are so screwed now! He'll kill you!

*(**YAGER** looks toward the ceiling.)*

YAGER. Shit. You're right. Got ya a present.

HOLLY. I don't want it.

YAGER. Yeah you do.

(He reaches into his backpack and pulls out a gift-wrapped box and gives it to **HOLLY**.*)*

HOLLY. I don't want it.

YAGER. C'mon! Open it up.

(Reluctantly, she does. It's a Monika doll.)

HOLLY. Wow. It's a Monika.

YAGER. You like it, right?

HOLLY. I can't believe you remembered. But she's so... expensive.

YAGER. Mom and Phil won't miss it. They've lost more than that at Foxwoods in ten minutes. I saw it happen.

(pause)

I *think* that was them. I was a little wasted.

DAD. *(from off)* Holly bear?

*(***YAGER** *kisses* **HOLLY** *quick.)*

YAGER. *(whispers)* I gotta go.

*(***YAGER** *starts to climb out of the window.)*

(whispers) You can't hide from life forever.

HOLLY. I was hiding from you.

YAGER. *(whispers)* You'll never escape your lover man.

DAD. *(from the top of the stairs, but not visible)* Holly? What's going on?

*(***YAGER** *is now out the window and looking back in.)*

YAGER. *(whispers)* Have you gained weight?

HOLLY. Yes.

YAGER. *(whispers)* Maybe you should try Pilates.

HOLLY. I'M PREGNANT!

(silence)

DAD. *(still off)* Uh...I know.

*(***YAGER** *stares at her, silently.)*

(off) Is everything OK?

HOLLY. I think so.

DAD. *(off)* I heard glass break.

HOLLY. It was nothing, Dad.

DAD. *(off)* You're not in your bare feet, are you?

HOLLY. No.

(pause)

DAD. *(off)* When are you gonna come back upstairs? This is silly.

HOLLY. I know.

DAD. *(off)* I miss you up here.

HOLLY. I'm gonna go to sleep now.

(pause)

DAD. Let me know if you need me. I'll be up here in the kitchen eatin' more cake. Just a holler away. Holly Hobby.

(After a moment the basement door closes.)

YAGER. *I* made you pregnant?

HOLLY. Yeah.

YAGER. How comes you didn't –

HOLLY. 'Cuz I didn't want you to know.

YAGER. But – But – I'm like the *Dad*! That's like responsibility.

HOLLY. You're nothing to me, Yager! Nothing! Why haven't you figured that out?! No wonder you got left back three years in a row!

YAGER. I did not! It was TWICE!

HOLLY. If I say I don't want to be with you, then that's it.

(silence)

YAGER. You never liked me much, did you?

*(**HOLLY** tries to hand the Monika doll to **YAGER** through the window.)*

HOLLY. I shouldn't keep this.

YAGER. *I* don't want it!

HOLLY. Here.

YAGER. Do you like it or not?

HOLLY. Yeah.

YAGER. Then just keep it.

HOLLY. OK.

YAGER. You're mad.

HOLLY. Yeah.

(silence)

YAGER. I'm sorry.

HOLLY. Do you know what you're sorry for?

YAGER. I didn't know you'd be so mad. Like for real mad.

HOLLY. Tell me what you're sorry for.

YAGER. I don't wanna say it.

HOLLY. You have to.

YAGER. *Why*?

HOLLY. Because you do.

(pause)

YAGER. I'm sorry I made you. Do it.
I am. *OK*?

(pause)

HOLLY. You have to pay for the window.

YAGER. Can I ever see it?

HOLLY. The window?

YAGER. The baby.

HOLLY. I don't want to discuss that with you.

YAGER. It's not fair.

HOLLY. Next time you'll know better.

YAGER. Can I ever see *you*?

HOLLY. You've seen me enough.

*(**YAGER** looks as though he might cry. But he won't.)*

YAGER. My Uncle Jake. He's had two heart attacks. And he got his foot hacked off 'cuz a the diabetes. And you know what? He still can drive a monster truck with no help at all. You don't know everything. You don't know what people can do. I may not always be…good. I'm not perfect. But I got stuff I'm good at. You don't know 'cuz you never asked. You never asked 'cuz you don't give a shit. I bet you I could be a good Dad. I just bet you.

I bet you. I bet you I'd be better at it than you.

*(**HOLLY** sighs but **YAGER** won't let her interrupt.)*

Have you ever even held a real baby?

(no response)

I have. I'm good at it.

I bet you you're gonna miss me.

HOLLY. Maybe. Why don't you go home and hop on one leg until I call?

*(**HOLLY** lays down on her bed and turns out the light.)*

YAGER. Happy birthday, Holly.

(He exits.)

Scene Twelve – Month 7

*(***HOLLY*** is trying to play a video game, but seems grumpy and disturbed. She picks up her Dasia® doll.)*

HOLLY. Hey, fatty.

(no response)

HOLLY. I'm supposed to be getting this miracle gift but… I should feel warm and full of God's love. I just feel hot and full of babies! You know?

(No response. She puts the doll down. She looks around.)

(to **BLACK DOLL 2***)* OK. I know you're mad at me. Just say it.

(no response)

Come on. I didn't *actually* torch you guys now, did I? What is your problem?

(From offstage, **DR. MCNUTHIN** *sighs loudly.)*

DR. MCNUTHIN. Come and get me.

*(***HOLLY*** goes to get her from the back, but is slower than normal.)*

Are you comin' or not?

HOLLY. It's a longer distance than it usedta be.

(Finally she makes it offstage and brings **DR. MCNUTHIN** *onstage, putting her in the chair.* **DR. MCNUTHIN** *clears her throat.)*

Oh yeah.

*(***HOLLY*** hands her glasses to her and then lays down.)*

I'm depressed. Make it go away.

DR. MCNUTHIN. I can't do that.

HOLLY. Well…can you call up Pastor Dave?

DR. MCNUTHIN. No.

HOLLY. Then what good are you? What can you do?

DR. MCNUTHIN. Nothing. I've never done anything before.

(**HOLLY** *considers this.*)

HOLLY. That's true. You really haven't.

DR. MCNUTHIN. No.

HOLLY. What's happening around here? Everything feels off.

DR. MCNUTHIN. I'll tell ya. But first you have to promise not to put me on Craig's List! Holly, I'm an old woman, I need my dignity.

HOLLY. *What*?!

DR. MCNUTHIN. Promise first!

HOLLY. Fine! I promise – *WHAT*?!

DR. MCNUTHIN. You're beyond us now.

HOLLY. I don't understand.

DR. MCNUTHIN. They ain't gonna talk no more. Not when they think a real flesh and blood doll is about to take their place. You made a choice. They tried to stop you from getting this far, but you sacrificed one of us. You damn-near sacrificed *all* of us. You'd do anything to protect those critters in your belly. It's ending.

HOLLY. That's the stupidest most medieval thing I've ever heard!

DR. MCNUTHIN. You wait and see. You'll be another person when it's all done.

HOLLY. Well what about you? Why are you still talking?

DR. MCNUTHIN. Fine print. Technically I'm a puppet. Not a doll. I have a little more autonomy.

(*pause*)

HOLLY. Will…will they ever talk again?

DR. MCNUTHIN. Not if you keep on maturing.

HOLLY. Demi talks to her dolls.

DR. MCNUTHIN. They don't talk back, puddin'. No exceptions to the rules. Even for the rich and famous.

(*pause*)

HOLLY. You know what I think?

DR. MCNUTHIN. What's that?

HOLLY. I think I'm no longer God's favorite.

Scene Thirteen – Month 8

*(**HOLLY** is pretty big now. She is alone in the basement. And her aloneness is pronounced. It's late at night and she can't sleep. **HOLLY** gets a bed sheet and a flashlight. She kneels.)*

HOLLY. Are you there God? It's me, Holly. Thanks for all of your blessings, which are plentiful. As you know. This will sound strange so brace yourself, but I don't always know if you're really listening. I hope you forgive me for what I suspect is a temporary questioning of my faith. I know it will return.

(She looks down at her big belly.)

Soon.

And – um – I think that there is a slight, microscopic chance, that I owe you an even bigger apology. I've been telling everyone that I've banished myself down here to please you. But you and I know that you never asked me to do any such thing. It's scary up there sometimes, God. I needed…a break.

(pause)

I know it's a sin, but I think about reincarnation sometimes. I can't lose them, God. I can't lose *both.* What if I give birth and it's my Mom? Reincarnated? That's weird. I know. But what if it happens? How would I know? What if she comes out, expects to see me and then – I'm not there? Can you give me a sign? Some kind of – guidance?

(pause)

Probably not.

You're not helping anyway, so…I'm gonna need you to forgive me for what I'm about to do. I can't explain it. The cravings. So please: Look away.

*(**HOLLY** turns on the flashlight and covers herself with the bed sheet. She begins to masturbate.)*

DR. MCNUTHIN. *(os)* Holly? If you need any inspiration I have a vintage *Playgirl* with Don Johnson as the centerfold. 'Course you probably don't know who he is.

(pause)

He was an actor on a popular crime drama from –

HOLLY. SHUT UP!

*(**HOLLY** continues for a few moments until the unmistakable sound of a woman moaning is heard from upstairs and then a voice saying: "SHHH!" **HOLLY** stops suddenly. She pulls the sheet down, revealing her face.)*

Dad?

*(Again, there is the distinct sound of a woman moaning and the bang of furniture. **HOLLY** marches up the stairs, opens the basement door and:)*

HOLLY. WHAT ARE YOU DOING?! I CAN TOTALLY –

*(Complete silence. After a moment, **HOLLY** runs down the stairs, looking pale. **DAD**, in boxers and a semi-buttoned shirt, races after her.)*

DAD. Holly…please. Calm down. Breathe a little. Take a breath for Daddy, please.

*(**HOLLY** glares at him.)*

That was sort of…an accident. Not an accident-accident, but a, it was –

Holly Hobby?

*(**HOLLY** doesn't respond.)*

Truth is, Holly, Daddy gets lonely sometimes. And… it really *was* a kind of an accident. I had no intention of doing that in the house. With you here. She just popped over and –

HOLLY. Tell me: What is her *real* job here? Was the tutoring just a cover up?

DAD. That's nasty, Holly.

HOLLY. This is all nasty, to me. You are such a sorry excuse for a father.

(pause)

DAD. I'm doing my best.

HOLLY. God sees you. So does Mom. You think "your best" is good enough for them?

(silence)

DAD. You are the most self-centered person I've ever known.

HOLLY. *Dad*?!

DAD. I am no longer gonna tip-toe around your whims. Now I'm sorry you saw what you saw. That probably counts as a trauma. But I'm not sorry for what I did. And I don't have to be.

HOLLY. You're a fornicator.

DAD. Newsflash, Bubble: So are you.

(pause)

HOLLY. I don't want her coming here anymore.

DAD. That's not up to you.

HOLLY. I won't listen to her.

DAD. Fine. Don't. You're only hurting yourself.

I hope eventually you forgive me. I hope you don't hold onto your anger until it rots your insides. That'd be bad for the twins.

HOLLY. I'll forgive you. Buy me a present?

DAD. *(with difficulty)* No. *No.*

(as if he's never said the word before) No no no no NO. It's so easy.

*(**DAD** starts up the stairs.)*

HOLLY. When you were my age, she wasn't even born yet. That's disgusting.

DAD. That's where you're wrong. She was three and a half months.

Goodnight.

(**DAD** *exits. Pause.*)

MIA. *(From the top of the stairs, unseen:)* I'm sorry, Holly. I hope this doesn't ruin our camaraderie. Remember? Woman to woman?

(**HOLLY** *doesn't respond.*)

Scene Fourteen – Month 9

*(**MIA** and **HOLLY** are in the basement. Again. **HOLLY** glares at **MIA** with her arms crossed.)*

MIA. It's math. You like math. Maybe even a little calculus. It'll be fun.

HOLLY. I'm not speaking to you.

MIA. You don't have to speak to do math problems.

HOLLY. I don't talk to whores.

MIA. Anyone ever tell you you're a mean piece a work?

HOLLY. I'm telling Dad you said that.

MIA. You think he doesn't know?

HOLLY. I hate you. You're not that smart. You're a mediocre teacher, at best. I bet you're not even a good fuck.

MIA. Your *mouth*! You need to start gargling with Clorox.

HOLLY. Average, average, *average.* That's all you are. Nothing special. I'm nothing like you! I'll always stand out in a crowd.

MIA. That's for damn sure.

HOLLY. That's why you're a slut. You're so boring, you'd just fade into the ether if you didn't spread your legs.

*(**MIA** slaps **HOLLY** across her face. **HOLLY** is shocked. So is **MIA**.)*

DR. MCNUTHIN. *(offstage)* Did I just hear a *bitch* slap? Is Ethel out there?

*(**HOLLY** opens her mouth, but before she can say anything, **MIA** slaps her again.)*

HOLLY. WHAT THE –

*(**MIA** slaps her again.)*

MIA. That really felt good!

HOLLY. DAAAAAAAAAAAAAAAAAAAAAAAAAAAAAAAAA AAAAAAAAD!

MIA. He's at the office.

HOLLY. Get me the phone, bitch!

MIA. *(giddy) You* get the phone. Bitch.

(Suddenly **HOLLY***'s face changes. She collapses into a chair.)*

HOLLY. Mia. Get me the phone.

MIA. *(even giddier)* Nope! Not gonna happen! I know I'm fired, but ya know what? I don't care! This is turnin' out to be a pretty good day.

HOLLY. Get me the phone!

MIA. Make me.

HOLLY. GODDAMMIT!

(silence)

I'm in labor! (God, forgive me.)

(Pause. **MIA** *races for the phone.)*

MIA. I should call 9-1-1.

HOLLY. Call my Dad.

MIA. 9-1-1.

HOLLY. *(Struggling through a contraction:)* Call your fuck buddy or I'll tear your face off, you cunt tube!!

*(***MIA** *dials the phone.)*

MIA. Hi, Dr. – uh, Greg? It's Mia. Yeah, I'm fine. I might have a sinus infection, but I –

HOLLY. *HELLO*?!

MIA. Oh! Holly's in labor.

*(***MIA** *hangs up.)*

We're gonna have to get you out of here.

HOLLY. Like Hell. (Sorry, God.)

MIA. You wanna get afterbirth all over the place?

*(***HOLLY** *ponders this when suddenly there is another crash at the window.* **YAGER** *has busted in again. A burglar alarm goes off this time.)*

YAGER. Oh, cool! That's loud!

HOLLY. GET OUT!!!

MIA. Oh my God! We're being robbed!

HOLLY. No! But you wouldn't say "*We're* being robbed," 'cuz *you* don't live here!

YAGER. Oh, shit! It's about to pop out, isn't it?

MIA. Who are you?

YAGER. Yager Meister, pretty lady! Whassup?!

HOLLY. Make him leave!

YAGER. I can't leave! I don't care what you say! My baby's about to be born.

*(**MIA**'s face darkens.)*

MIA. You son of a bitch!

YAGER. Whoa! Calm down, sister.

MIA. You son of a –

*(**MIA** gives **YAGER** a swift front kick to the chest – a righteous kickboxing move – sending him to the floor.)*

He's subdued. For the moment.

HOLLY. *(smiling through a contraction:)* You're violent today.

MIA. Shit! I know. Sorry.

HOLLY. *(still struggling)* No. You're – sort of – awesome.

*(**MIA** smiles, tries to put her arm around **HOLLY**, but **HOLLY** smacks her hand away. **DAD** enters, racing down the stairs.)*

DAD. Bubble? Baby? You timing the, the…things?

HOLLY. No. But they're comin' pretty fast.

*(**YAGER** starts to cough from the ground.)*

DAD. You.

You little bastard! Did you break *another* window?

YAGER. *(struggling to get to his feet)* Oh man! I'm sorry, sir. I haveta . . .

*(**YAGER** tries to escape, but **DAD** grabs him, picks him up and brings him back.)*

DAD. We have lots and *lots* to talk about, young man.

*(**YAGER** is terrified.)*

Later. First, you're gonna help us get her out of here.

HOLLY. Daddy no –

DAD. Holly Bear, don't be difficult. I have chloroform. Don't make me use it.

HOLLY. DAD!

*(***HOLLY** *grabs* **DR. MCNUTHIN***.)*

I can walk.

*(***DAD** *and* **MIA** *help* **HOLLY** *up to the stairs.* **YAGER** *watches helplessly.)*

YAGER. Can I help?

HOLLY. Yager, go home.

YAGER. But I got skills.

DAD. *(Warning:)* Yager!

YAGER. Don't I have any rights?

HOLLY / MIA / DAD. GO HOME!

(They exit. Outside we hear the sound of a car starting up. **YAGER** *picks up a few dolls.)*

YAGER. *(ss one of the dolls)* Your mama is *so* dumb . . .

*(***YAGER** *tries to think of a punchline. He's really thinking.)*

Awwwww man these are hard.

(He's still thinking as we hear the sound of the car revving outside. It doesn't start. A moment. Then **DAD** *appears at the top of the stairs.)*

DAD. All right, dumbass. We need you to drive.

*(***YAGER** *exits in triumph. There is a moment of complete silence. The basement is still. None of the dolls talk or move. It is eerie and a little sad.)*

Scene Fifteen

(One week later. Springtime. **HOLLY***'s backyard. There are some dandelions or wild daisies or sunflowers – something extreme to indicate the beauty of spring. From a doorway,* **DAD** *enters. He then looks behind him, waiting.)*

DAD. Almost there. Just a few more steps.

(Slowly **HOLLY** *emerges, holding* **DR. MCNUTHIN**. *She seems small and frail; just a kid.)*

You did it! All by yourself, too.

(pause)

It's a beautiful day. Must be 78 degrees at least. Nice little breeze. Must be nice to feel that on your skin, huh?

(no response)

You've been so quiet. It's a little jarring actually. Been almost a week since . . .

(no response)

I'm sorry, Holly. I hope the adult in you knows that. It's not right to separate twins. It's unnatural.

(a little regret) They were adorable, weren't they?

(no response)

I know you don't believe me, but I pray, too.

*(***HOLLY** *looks at* **DAD***.)*

DAD. I pray to your Mom. I ask her for help. Raising you is not easy. What do I know about little girls? Adolescent girls. *Pubescent* girls. When you told me...what happened? I could've just spent the next nine months weeping, Holly Bear. Sometimes I did.

(still no response)

I didn't do a perfect job with you. That's as clear as Waterford. But I hope I didn't...screw you up. I worry about that all the time.

HOLLY. You didn't.

DAD. It's not really for you to say, though, is it?

HOLLY. No.

I'm sorry, too.

DAD. What for?

HOLLY. I don't know. I just am.

DAD. You look different.

HOLLY. Do I look old? 'Cuz I feel old. Like I feel like I have wrinkles. Do I have wrinkles?

(**DAD** *smiles. They do NOT hug or kiss or anything like that right now.)*

DAD. I don't think so.

(He picks up **DR. MCNUTHIN** *and examines her.)*

Now *this* thing is gettin' old. Maybe we can take her to a refiner? Get her fixed up?

(**HOLLY** *shakes her head and takes* **DR. MCNUTHIN** *back.)*

HOLLY. I like her like this.

DAD. I should get back to work. I feel bad leaving . . .

HOLLY. I'm fine, Dad.

I mean – I will be fine.

(**DAD** *starts to exit. He turns around.)*

DAD. From now on…I'm just gonna call you Holly. Plain and simple. No more cutesy stuff. Is that all right?

(**HOLLY** *gives a near-smile.* **DAD** *exits.)*

HOLLY. *(to* **DR. MCNUTHIN***)* Sorry he grabbed you like that.

(No response. **HOLLY** *becomes frightened.)*

Et tu??? Where have you gone?

(no response)

What happened to the fine print?

(No response. **HOLLY** *become momentarily angry, then she softens and clutches the doll.)*

Hey God? Can you help me? Can you please help me to be……OK. And? Can you help me find some friends? Maybe? I understand the finer points of the Doppler Effect. I should be able to get people to like me.

(pause)

Take care of the twins.

A-men.

*(**MIA** cautiously enters. She sits next to **HOLLY** on the grass. **DR. MCNUTHIN** sits between them.)*

MIA. How're you feeling?

HOLLY. All right.

MIA. I'm so sorry I hit you. That was completely inappropriate. Outrageously inappropriate. I'm a terrible tutor.

HOLLY. I forgot about that.

MIA. Then I'm sorry I brought it up.

(pause)

HOLLY. You still fucking him?

MIA. Holly?!

HOLLY. Are you?

MIA. Are you still born-again?

(pause)

No. He ended it. It was too weird for him. He's pretty conventional.

HOLLY. Why are you here? 'Cuz a him?

MIA. No. I just told you –

HOLLY. Then why are you here?

MIA. Do you want me to leave?

HOLLY. I want you to answer my question.

*(**MIA** thinks about **HOLLY**'s question.)*

MIA. You're me. Younger…me.

HOLLY. I don't think so.

MIA. Oh, but I do.

HOLLY. *(a bit flattered)* Really?

MIA. I think you're like my personal koan. I can't move onto the next phase of my life until I figure you out. I met this guy that's into Japanese Zen Buddhism, but that's another discussion.

HOLLY. Does that mean I'm someone you would spend time with? If you weren't being...paid?

MIA. There's something to be said for bratty little sisters.

(pause)

HOLLY. When you lose something so big, how do you keep going?

MIA. It's really, *really* hard.

And then after a while, it's kind of hard. And then mildly hard. And then just hard. Maybe time keeps compressing the loss until it's easy. Though I doubt it. But I don't know the definitive answer. I'm really not that wise.

HOLLY. *(unintentional insult)* That's true.

MIA. But there's one thing I DO know.

(Suddenly, **MIA** *picks up* **DR. MCNUTHIN**, *which alarms* **HOLLY**.*)*

HOLLY. She's not gonna like that!

MIA. *(She sings the second half of the first verse of "Diamonds are a Girls Best Friend" by Marilyn Monroe while manipulating* **DR. MCNUTHIN**.* *)*

A KISS ON THE HAND MAY BE QUITE CONTINENTAL...

(Pause; **HOLLY** *stares at* **DR. MCNUTHIN** *in amazement, as though she can't believe this is happening.* **MIA** *continues to sing the second, third, and fourth verses of* Diamonds Are A Girls Best Friend.** *)*

*(***HOLLY** *laughs.)*

---

* Please see Music Use Note on page 3.

** Please see Music Use Note on page 3

MIA. God I have been **DYING** to do that for months! *And* I made you laugh! I knew it was possible!

*(**HOLLY** grabs **DR. MCNUTHIN** and looks at her with new eyes.)*

HOLLY. *(As though surprised:)* She didn't mind at all.

*(**MIA** takes her back.)*

MIA. This is dedicated to my favorite born-again Christian!

*(Sings the first few lines of "Jesus is Just Alright" by , while manipulating **DR. MCNUTHIN**.*)*

JESUS IS JUST ALRIGHT WITH ME...

HOLLY. HEY!

(A scary silence. Then:)

My turn!

*(**HOLLY** takes the doll and energetically sings the first verse of "Milkshake" by Kelis.**)*

MY MILKSHAKE BRINGS ALL THE BOYS TO THE YARD...

MIA. Whoa! I don't know if Jesus would approve.

*(**HOLLY** shrugs.)*

HOLLY. I...think He can handle it.

End of Play

---

* Please see Music Use note on page 3

** Please see Music Use Note on page 3